HATCHIMALS™

D0774720

PUFFIN BOOKS

UK | USA | Canada | Ireland | Australia
India | New Zealand | South Africa

Puffin Books is part of the Penguin Random House group of companies
whose addresses can be found at global.penguinrandomhouse.com.

www.penguin.co.uk
www.puffin.co.uk
www.ladybird.co.uk

Penguin
Random House
UK

First published 2018
001

Written by Lauren Holowaty

Printed in Great Britain by Clays Ltd, St Ives plc

A CIP catalogue record for this book is available from the British Library

ISBN: 978–0–241–32163–8

All correspondence to:
Puffin Books
Penguin Random House Children's
80 Strand, London WC2R 0RL

MIX

Penguin Random House is committed to a

HATCHiMALS™

EGGcellent JOKe BOOK

PUFFIN

WELCOME TO HATCHTOPIA!

Hey there! I'm Giggling Penguala, Hatchtopia's best practical joker!

This book is full of eggs-tremely funny gags about the Hatchimals families and our favourite hangouts. You'll soon have your friends giggling all the way to Giggle Grove!

CONTENTS

LET'S GET CRACKING!

WHAT DID THE HATCHIMALS EGG SAY WHEN IT WAS LOOKING FOR ADVENTURE?

'LET'S HATCH A PLAN!'

WHY CAN'T YOU MAKE FUN OF EGGS?

THEY CAN'T TAKE A YOLK!

WHAT DID THE OTHER HATCHIMALS EGG SAY IN REPLY?

'OK. I MIGHT WHISK IT!'

WHAT DID ONE HATCHIMALS EGG SAY TO THE OTHER?

LET'S GET CRACKING!

WHAT DO YOU CALL A TIRED HATCHIMALS EGG?

EGGS-HAUSTED!

WHAT DO YOU CALL AN EGG FROM OUTER SPACE?

An EGGS-TRATERRESTRIAL!

WHAT DO HATCHIMALS EGGS DO TO KEEP FIT?

EGGS-ERCISE!

WHAT ARE GEGS?

SCRAMBLED EGGS!

HOW DID THE HATCHIMALS EGG CROSS THE ROAD?

IT SCRAMBLED ACROSS!

WHAT DO YOU CALL SOMEONE WHO COLLECTS HATCHIMALS EGGS?

A COLL-EGG-TOR!

WHAT DID ONE HATCHIMALS EGG SAY TO THE OTHER WHEN HE THOUGHT SHE WASN'T LISTENING?

'DON'T EGG-NORE ME!'

WHY ARE HATCHIMALS EGGS LAID?

BECAUSE IF THEY WERE DROPPED, THEY'D BREAK!

GARDEN

The Garden is the perfect place to plant the seed of something silly! The Garden Hatchimals like nothing better than nestling in among the Dazzling Daisies and telling jokes to make one another laugh.

WHY DOES YELLOW BEEBULL HAVE STICKY HAIR?

BECAUSE SHE USES A HONEYCOMB!

WHY DO SOME MOUSESWIFTS NEED OILING?

BECAUSE THEY SQUEAK!

WHAT DO YOU CALL MAGENTA MOUSESWIFT WITH CARROTS IN HER EARS?

ANYTHING – SHE CAN'T HEAR YOU!

WHY DID BLUE FROWL INVITE FRIENDS OVER TO HIS GARDEN?

BECAUSE HE DIDN'T WANT TO BE OWL BY HIMSELF!

WHAT KIND OF BOOK DOES YELLOW BUNWEE LIKE TO READ?

ONE WITH A HOPPY ENDING!

WHAT DO YOU CALL A SLEEPING BEEBULL?

A BULL-DOZER!

WHAT DO YOU CALL A MACOW WHO HELPS OUT IN THE GARDEN?

A LAWN MOO-ER!

WHAT DO YOU CALL A FROWL WITH A LOW VOICE?

A GROWL!

WHAT KIND OF BEAN NEVER GROWS IN A GARDEN?

A JELLY BEAN!

PINK BUTTERPUFF: KNOCK, KNOCK!
BLUE DRAGONFLIP: WHO'S THERE?
PINK BUTTERPUFF: PICKLE.
BLUE DRAGONFLIP: PICKLE WHO?
PINK BUTTERPUFF: PICKLE LITTLE FLOWER AND GIVE IT TO YOUR FRIEND!

HOW DO SNAILTAILS GET THEIR SHELLS SO SHINY?

THEY USE SNAIL POLISH!

WHY IS GREEN SNAILTAIL SO STRONG?

BECAUSE HE CARRIES HIS HOUSE ON HIS BACK!

WHAT KIND OF PARTY DID MAGENTA MOUSESWIFT HAVE WHEN SHE MOVED HOUSE?

A MOUSE-WARMING PARTY!

WHO IS YELLOW BEEBULL'S FAVOURITE COMPOSER?

Bee-THOVEN!

WHAT GETS BIGGER THE MORE YOU TAKE AWAY?

A HOLE IN THE GARDEN!

WHAT IS BLUE MOUSESWIFT'S FAVOURITE GAME?

HIDE-AND-SQUEAK!

WHICH GARDEN INSECT IS THE MOST MUSICAL?

A HUMBUG!

WHAT DID YELLOW BEEBULL SAY TO THE FLOWER?

HI, HONEY!

WHICH FLOWERS TELL THE BEST JOKES?

SILLY LILIES!

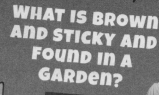

WHAT IS BROWN AND STICKY AND FOUND IN A GARDEN?

A STICK!

WHAT HAPPENS WHEN A SNAILTAIL LOSES ITS SHELL?

IT BEGINS TO FEEL SLUGGISH!

WHY DID PINK BEEBULL PUT HONEY UNDER HER PILLOW?

SHE WANTED SWEET DREAMS!

WHAT DOES YELLOW MOUSESWIFT LIKE FOR BREAKFAST?

MICE CRISPIES!

BLUE DRAGONFLIP: KNOCK, KNOCK!
GREEN FROWL: WHO'S THERE?
BLUE DRAGONFLIP: BUTTER.
GREEN FROWL: BUTTER WHO?
BLUE DRAGONFLIP: BUTTERPUFF!

13

FARM

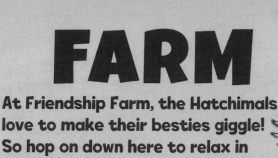

At Friendship Farm, the Hatchimals
love to make their besties giggle!
So hop on down here to relax in
the Honey Hay and try out some
of these farm-tastic funnies.
They're bound to *grow* on you!

**HOW DO ORANGE
CHICKCHAFF AND
RED CHICKCHAFF
GET STRONG?**

THEY EGG-CERSISE!

WHAT DO YOU GET WHEN A HATCHIMALS EGG IS ON TOP OF A BARN?

AN EGG ROLL!

WHAT DO YOU CALL A LAMBLET COVERED IN CHOCOLATE?

A CHOCOLATE BAA!

WHERE SHOULD YOU TAKE PINK PONETTE IF SHE'S SICK?

HORSE-PITAL!

WHY DIDN'T ANYONE LAUGH AT RED CHICKCHAFF'S JOKES?

BECAUSE THEY WERE TOO CORNY!

HOW DOES A FARMER COUNT MACOWS?

USING A MACOW-CULATOR!

WHY IS THE BARN AT FRIENDSHIP FARM SO NOISY?

BECAUSE THE MACOWS HAVE HORNS!

WHAT DID THE HATCHIMALS SAY WHEN THEY FORGOT TO PLANT THE CORN?

'AW, SHUCKS!'

WHERE DO PINK LAMBLET AND BLUE LAMBLET WASH?

IN THE BAA-TH!

WHO TELLS JOKES ABOUT CHICKCHAFFS?

COMEDI-HENS!

WHERE DID THE LAMBLET GET A HAIRCUT?

THE BAA-BAA SHOP!

WHY ARE CHICKCHAFFS FORTUNATE?

NO REASON - THEY'RE JUST CLUCKY!

WHAT DO YOU CALL BLUE PONETTE WHEN HE LIVES NEXT DOOR?

YOUR NEIGH-BOUR!

WHAT DO YOU CALL AN EXCITED CHICKCHAFF?

HEN-THUSIASTIC!

DID YOU HEAR ABOUT THE MAGIC TRACTOR?

IT WENT DOWN THE ROAD AND TURNED INTO A FIELD!

WHAT DO YOU GIVE BLUE PONETTE WHEN HE HAS A COLD?

COUGH STIRRUP!

ORANGE MACOW: KNOCK, KNOCK!
BLUE DONKEMU: WHO'S THERE?
ORANGE MACOW: COWS GO.
BLUE DONKEMU: COWS GO WHO?
ORANGE MACOW: COWS GO 'MOO'!

WHAT DO YOU CALL BLUE LAMBLET WHEN HE'S DANCING?

A BAA-LLERINA!

WHAT DO WHITE MACOW AND ORANGE MACOW LIKE DANCING TO?

ANY MOO-SIC AT ALL!

HOW DID BLUE LAMBLET FIND ORANGE MACOW ON FRIENDSHIP FARM?

HE TRACTOR DOWN!

WHAT DID ORANGE MACOW SAY TO WHITE MACOW?

'MOOOO-VE OVER!'

WHAT IS BLUE PONETTE'S FAVOURITE SPORT?

STABLE TENNIS!

WHERE DO YOU FIND OUT MORE ABOUT EGGS?

IN A HEN-CYCLOPEDIA!

WHAT DO YOU GET WHEN YOU CROSS A CHICKCHAFF WITH AN ALARM CLOCK?

AN ALARM CLUCK!

WHAT DO YOU CALL A STOLEN HATCHIMALS EGG?

A POACHED EGG!

WHAT VEGETABLE CAN TIE YOUR STOMACH IN KNOTS?

STRING BEANS!

'DOCTOR, DOCTOR, I FEEL LIKE A NIGHTINGOAT.'

'STOP BLEATING ON ABOUT IT!'

MEADOW

Cartwheel through the grass and join a game of Hatchy Ball down at the Meadow! Spring along to this sweet-smelling place and you're bound to see a big smile on everyone's faces. Especially after you tell them these jokes!

WHAT IS GREEN HEDGYHEN'S FAVOURITE FLAVOUR OF CRISPS?

PRICKLED ONION!

WHAT DID YELLOW KITTYCAN SAY WHEN SHE DROPPED HER BOUQUET IN THE MEADOW?

WHOOPSY DAISIES!

WHAT DO YOU CALL A FROZEN PUPPIT?

A PUP-SICLE!

WHAT DO YOU CALL A PUPPIT EGG?

A POOCHED EGG!

WHAT DO YOU GET WHEN YOU CROSS BLUE PUPPIT WITH A CALCULATOR?

A FRIEND YOU CAN COUNT ON!

WHAT DID YELLOW KITTYCAN WEAR TO BED?

PAW-JAMAS!

WHAT DO YOU GET WHEN YOU CROSS GREEN HEDGYHEN WITH A BALLOON?

A LOUD POP!

WHY DID BLUE KITTYCAN THINK THE MEADOW'S GRASS MIGHT BE DANGEROUS?

BECAUSE SHE HEARD IT'S FULL OF BLADES!

WHAT IS YELLOW KITTYCAN'S FAVOURITE COLOUR?

PURR-PLE!

WHAT DID PINK HEDGYHEN SAY WHEN HE PUT HIS COAT ON INSIDE OUT?

'OW!'

21

WHAT DO YOU CALL A PAINTING OF A KITTYCAN?

A PAW-TRAIT!

HOW DOES PURPLE PUPPIT SWIM WHEN HE VISITS LILAC LAKE?

DOGGIE-PADDLE!

WHY DID BLUE KITTYCAN RUN AWAY FROM THE TREE?

SHE WAS AFRAID OF ITS BARK!

WHAT DO GREEN HEDGYHEN AND PINK HEDGYHEN SAY WHEN THEY HUG EACH OTHER?

'OUCH!'

WHY DID THE MEADOW GO TO THE DOCTOR?

IT WAS LOOKING GREEN!

WHAT IS PURPLE PUPPIT'S FAVOURITE MUSICAL INSTRUMENT?

THE TROM-Bone!

WHY DOESN'T BLUE KITTYCAN LIKE GOING SHOPPING?

SHE PREFERS ORDERING FROM CAT-ALOGUES!

WHY DID BLUE PUPPIT STAY IN THE SHADE?

SO HE DIDN'T TURN INTO A HOT DOG!

WHAT IS PURPLE PUPPIT'S FAVOURITE TYPE OF BOOK?

A PUP-UP BOOK!

WHY DO KITTYCANS MAKE GREAT FRIENDS?

BECAUSE THEY'RE PURR-FECT!

JUNGLE

Tell these jokes as you swing through the tropical trees and you'll soon cause a rumble in the Jungle! The Jungle Hatchimals are full of energy and love to play silly games. The next few pages will make this family of Hatchimals wild with laughter!

WHAT DO YOU CALL PURPLE PANDOR WHEN SHE'S CONFUSED?
BAMBOO-ZLED!

WHAT DID THE BANANA SAY TO PINK MONKIWI?
NOTHING - BANANAS CAN'T TALK!

HOW DID PINK MONKIWI GET DOWN THE STAIRS?
HE SLID DOWN THE BANANA-STER!

WHAT COLOUR SOCKS DOES BLUE PANDOR WEAR?
SHE DOESN'T WEAR SOCKS - SHE HAS BEAR FEET!

24

WHAT'S PURPLE GORILLABEE'S FAVOURITE TYPE OF BISCUIT?

CHOCOLATE CHIMP!

WHAT DO YOU CALL BLUE TIGRETTE WHEN HE'S PLAYING 'HATCHIMAL SAYS'?

A COPYCAT!

WHAT HAPPENED WHEN THE BANANA SAW BLUE MONKIWI?

THE BANANA SPLIT!

WHAT'S BLUE GORILLABEE'S FAVOURITE FRUIT?

APE-RICOT!

WHY DID PINK MONKIWI LIKE THE BANANA?

BECAUSE IT HAD APPEAL!

WHERE DO BLUE GORILLABEE AND PURPLE GORILLABEE GET THEIR GOSSIP IN THE JUNGLE?

ON THE APE VINE!

WHERE DO THE JUNGLE HATCHIMALS GO WHEN THEY LOSE THEIR TAILS?

TO A RE-TAIL PARK!

HOW DO PANDORS KEEP THEIR HOMES COOL IN SUMMER?

THEY USE BEAR CONDITIONING!

WHAT DID YELLOW CHAMELOON SAY WHEN SHE STOOD IN FRONT OF A PANE OF GLASS?

'HAVE I MADE MYSELF CLEAR?'

FOREST

Roam between the cool Orchard Pines and lovely Lavender Oaks and you'll soon discover a Forest full of Hatchimals ready to laugh their way to the treetops!

WHY DID THE FOREST TREES GET INTO TROUBLE?

BECAUSE THEY WERE BEING KNOTTY!

WHY IS PURPLE SKUNKLE SO CLEVER?

BECAUSE SHE HAS A LOT OF SCENTS!

WHAT DO YOU CALL A SMART GROUP OF TREES?

A BRAIN-FOREST!

HOW DO YOU CATCH A CHIPADEE IN THE FOREST?

CLIMB UP A TREE AND ACT LIKE A NUT!

WHY COULDN'T ORANGE CHIPADEE EAT A BRAZIL NUT?

IT WAS A TOUGH NUT TO CRACK!

WHICH TREE LOVES TO PLAY BOARD GAMES?

A CHESS-NUT TREE!

WHAT DID ORANGE BEAVEERY SAY TO THE TREE AFTER VISITING THE FOREST?

'IT'S BEEN NICE GNAWING YOU!'

WHAT DID THE TREE DO WHEN THE BANK CLOSED?

IT OPENED A NEW BRANCH!

WHY WAS PINK CHIPADEE LATE FOR SCHOOL?

THE TRAFFIC WAS NUTS!

WHAT DO YOU CALL BLUE DEERALOO WITH NO EYES?

NO I-DEER-ALOO!

WHAT DO YOU CALL BLUE DEERALOO WITH NO EYES AND NO WINGS?

STILL NO I-DEER-ALOO!

WHAT DO YOU CALL AN OWLING DRESSED AS A MAGICIAN?

HOOOO-DINI!

WHAT DID PINK OWLING SAY WHEN IT WAS RAINING?

'TOO WET TO WOO!'

WHAT HAPPENED WHEN PINK OWLING LOST HER VOICE?

SHE DIDN'T GIVE A HOOT!

HOW DO YOU EXPLAIN WHAT AN ACORN IS, USING VERY FEW WORDS?

IN A NUTSHELL, IT'S AN OAK TREE!

WHAT IS RED FOXFIN'S FAVOURITE DANCE?

THE FOXTROT!

WHAT DO YOU CALL A FLYING SKUNKLE?

A SMELL-ICOPTER!

HAVE YOU HEARD THE JOKE ABOUT PURPLE SKUNKLE?

DON'T BOTHER – IT STINKS!

WHY DOES PURPLE HUMMINGBEAR HUM?

BECAUSE SHE DOESN'T KNOW THE WORDS!

WHAT DID PURPLE MOOSEBEAK SAY ON A BUSY DAY IN THE FOREST?

'MOOSE ALONG, PLEASE!'

OCEAN

Welcome to the Ocean, where you can really make a splash. There's so much to 'sea' here! Get it? No? Maybe you're better off reading on to find a funnier Ocean joke . . .

WHAT KIND OF EGG LIVES BY THE OCEAN?

AN EGG SHELL!

WHY DID RED CRABLER CROSS THE ROAD?

TO GET TO THE OTHER TIDE!

WHAT RUNS BUT NEVER GETS TIRED?

WATER!

WHY DID TEAL DOLFINCH BLUSH?

BECAUSE HE SAW THE OCEAN'S BOTTOM!

WHY DO SOME PENGUALAS LIVE IN SALT WATER?

BECAUSE PEPPER MAKES THEM SNEEZE!

HOW DOES YELLOW CRABLER PHONE HER FRIENDS?

SHE USES HER SHELL PHONE!

WHY DID THE SAND AT THE BEACH GET WET?

BECAUSE THE SEA WEED!

WHAT DID PINK SEASPOON SAY TO BLUE SEASPOON?

'SEA YA LATER!'

HOW CAN YOU TELL THE OCEAN IS FRIENDLY?

BECAUSE IT WAVES!

WHY WOULDN'T RED CRABLER SHARE HIS DINNER WITH PINK OCTAPITTA?

BECAUSE HE WAS BEING A LITTLE SHELLFISH!

WHY DID YELLOW CRABLER GET CROSS WITH HER FRIENDS?

SHE WAS FEELING CRABBY!

WHERE DOES MAGENTA PENGUALA WATCH MOVIES?

AT THE DIVE-IN!

WHAT DOES MAGENTA PENGUALA DRINK FROM?

A BEAKER!

DID YOU KNOW THAT CRABLERS CAN SQUIRT INK?

ONLY SQUIDDING!

WHERE DOES YELLOW CRABLER SLEEP?

IN A WATER BED!

WHAT KIND OF SEA CREATURE ONLY COMES OUT AT NIGHT?

A STARFISH!

HOW DID BLUE OCTAPITTA MAKE PINK SEASPOON LAUGH?

WITH TEN-TICKLES!

WHAT DID ONE WAVE SAY TO THE OTHER?

NOTHING, IT JUST WAVED!

WHAT PARTY GAME DOES TEAL DOLFINCH LIKE TO PLAY?

SALMON SAYS!

WHAT DOESN'T GET WETTER WHEN IT RAINS?

THE OCEAN!

HOW DO PINK DOLFINCH AND BLUE DOLFINCH MAKE DECISIONS?

THEY FLIPPER COIN!

WHAT DOES
BLUE SEASPOON
TAKE TO STAY
HEALTHY?

VITAMIN SEA!

WHAT DOES
PINK OCTAPITTA
WEAR WHEN IT
GETS COLD?

**A COAT OF
ARMS!**

WHAT DID BLUE
OCTAPITTA SAY WHEN
MAGENTA PENGUALA
SUGGESTED GOING
FOR A DIP?

'WATER GOOD
IDEA!'

WHAT DID
TEAL DOLFINCH DO
WHEN YELLOW
CRABLER WAS LATE?

HE FLIPPED!

WHAT DID RED
CRABLER SAY
WHEN ASKED
HOW MUCH SALT
HE WANTED IN
HIS FOOD?

'JUST A PINCH!'

WHAT GETS WETTER THE MORE IT DRIES?

A BEACH TOWEL!

WHY DOES MAGENTA PENGUALA CARRY FISH IN HIS BEAK?

BECAUSE HE DOESN'T HAVE ANY POCKETS!

WHAT DO YOU MEASURE DOLFINCHES IN?

FEET AND FINCHES!

HOW WOULD YOU CUT THE OCEAN IN HALF?

WITH A SEA-SAW!

WHAT'S PINK OCTAPITTA'S FAVOURITE SNACK?

PITTA BREAD!

WHICH SIDE OF MAGENTA PENGUALA HAS THE MOST FEATHERS?

THE OUTSIDE!

SAVANNAH

It's *plain* to see that if you eggs-plore the Savannah you'll soon be roaring with laughter! The Savannah Hatchimals love travelling, and they've picked up plenty of hilarious jokes from all across Hatchtopia . . .

WHAT DOES YELLOW GIRREO CALL HER BOAT?

THE GIR-RAFT!

WHY ARE DRAGGLES GREAT STORYTELLERS?

THEY ALL HAVE TAILS!

HOW DO ELEFLIES TALK TO EACH OTHER?

`OVER THE ELEPHONE!`

WHAT DO YOU GET WHEN PINK GIRREO AND YELLOW GIRREO CRASH INTO EACH OTHER?

`A GIRAFFIC JAM!`

WHAT DO YOU CALL A ZEBRUSH SWIMMING UNDER WATER?

`A SEA-BRUSH!`

WHAT DO YOU GET IF YOU CROSS A TURTLE WITH PURPLE GIRREO?

`A PURPLE TURTLE-NECK!`

WHERE DOES GREEN ELEFLY KEEP HIS LUGGAGE?

`IN HIS TRUNK!`

`PINK GIRREO: KNOCK, KNOCK!`
`BLUE RHOOBY: WHO'S THERE?`
`PINK GIRREO: GIRAFFE.`
`BLUE RHOOBY: GIRAFFE WHO?`
`PINK GIRREO: GIRAFFE ANYTHING TO EAT? I'M HUNGRY!`

WHY DIDN'T ORANGE CHEETREE WANT TO CROSS THE ROAD?

BECAUSE SHE DIDN'T WANT TO GET SPOTTED!

WHAT'S YELLOW, SPOTTY AND GOES ROUND AND ROUND?

YELLOW CHEETREE IN A REVOLVING DOOR!

WHY DOES PINK DRAGGLE HAVE GREAT EYESIGHT?

BECAUSE SHE HAS AN EAGLE EYE!

WHAT DOES PINK LEORIOLE THINK OF THE SAVANNAH?

SHE THINKS IT'S ROARSOME!

WHY DO ELEFLIES HAVE TRUNKS?

BECAUSE THEY WOULD LOOK SILLY CARRYING SUITCASES!

WHAT'S THE DIFFERENCE BETWEEN AN INJURED LEORIOLE AND A WET DAY?

ONE ROARS WITH PAIN, THE OTHER POURS WITH RAIN!

WHAT EATS MORE FOOD THAN ONE RHOOBY?

TWO OF THEM!

WHAT DO YOU CALL AN ELEFLY THAT NEVER WASHES?

A SMELLY-FLY!

WHAT IS HUNGRY PURPLE RHOOBY'S FAVOURITE DAY OF THE WEEK?

CHEWS-DAY!

WHAT'S GREEN ELEFLY'S FAVOURITE SPORT?

SQUASH!

WHAT DOES PINK DRAGGLE LIKE TO SNACK ON?

FIRECRACKERS!

WHAT WOULD YOU CALL A ZEBRUSH IN A HURRY?

A ZEB-RUSHER!

41

DESERT

It's time to head to the Desert, where it's blazing hot in the day and super cool at night. If you *wallaby* funny, try and impress this Hatchimal family with some of these jokes!

WHY DID THE SANDSNAKE CROSS THE DESERT?

TO GET TO THE OTHER *SSSSSSSSSSIDE!*

WHAT DO YOU CALL THE DESERT WHEN NO HATCHIMALS ARE THERE?

DESERTED!

WHAT DOES GREEN SANDSNAKE LIKE BEFORE SHE GOES TO SLEEP?

A GOODNIGHT HISS!

WHAT MUSIC DOES BLUE KANGAROOSE LISTEN TO?

HIP-HOP!

HOW DID BLUE KANGAROOSE GET BETTER WHEN SHE WAS INJURED?

SHE HAD A HOP-ERATION!

WHY ISN'T BLUE KOALABEE A REAL BEAR?

HE DOESN'T HAVE THE RIGHT KOALA-FICATIONS!

WHAT DID BLUE KANGAROOSE SAY WHEN SHE WAS OFFERING PURPLE KANGAROOSE A PIGGYBACK?

'HOP ON!'

WHAT DO YOU CALL A BABY KANGAROOSE WHEN IT'S FEELING A BIT LAZY?

A POUCH POTATO!

WHAT DOES PURPLE KANGAROOSE LIKE TO EAT?

LOLLI-HOPS!

WHAT IS MAGENTA CAMELARK'S FAVOURITE NURSERY RHYME?

'HUMPTY DUMPTY!'

WHAT IS OUT OF BOUNDS IN THE DESERT?

A TIRED PURPLE KANGAROOSE!

HOW DOES YELLOW CAMELARK HIDE HERSELF?

CAMEL-FLAGE!

WHAT ARE BLUE SANDSNAKE'S FAVOURITE MAGIC WORDS?

ADDER-CA-DABRA!

WHAT DO HATCHIMALS LIKE TO EAT IN THE DESERT?

DESSERT!

44

WHY IS GREEN SANDSNAKE HARD TO FOOL?

YOU CAN'T PULL HER LEG!

WHAT DOES GREEN SANDSNAKE DO WHEN SHE WRITES A LETTER?

SEALS IT WITH A HISS!

WHY DOESN'T GREEN SANDSNAKE NEED TO WEIGH HERSELF?

BECAUSE SHE HAS HER OWN SCALES!

WHAT DO YOU SAY WHEN GREEN ARMADILLARK IS MESSING AROUND?

'SHE'S LARKING ABOUT!'

WHAT DID GREEN SANDSNAKE SAY WHEN SHE DID SOMETHING WRONG?

'SORRY, MY MISSSSSSSSTAKE!'

RIVER

Lounge about, lie back and have a laugh with the River Hatchimals, who are famous throughout Hatchtopia for their sense of humour. These Hatchimals are playful, funny and love a good joke – so tell a few of these and you'll soon be making a splash!

WHERE DO RIVER HATCHIMALS KEEP THEIR MONEY?

IN A RIVERBANK!

WHAT TIME OF DAY DOES GREEN DUCKLE WAKE UP?

AT THE QUACK OF DAWN!

WHAT DO DUCKLES EAT WITH CHEESE?

QUACKERS!

WHAT DOES BLUE DUCKLE CARRY HER SCHOOLBOOKS IN?

HER QUACK-PACK!

WHAT DID BLUE DUCKLE SAY WHEN THE WAITRESS CAME?

'CAN YOU PUT IT ON MY BILL, PLEASE?'

WHAT DO YOU CALL A FIDGETY PIGEON?

A FIGEON!

WHAT DOES RED SWOTTER DO WHEN IT RAINS?

SHE GETS WET!

WHAT DOES TEAL BEAVEERY EAT FOR BREAKFAST?

OAK-MEAL!

WHAT DO YOU GIVE BLUE FIGEON WHEN HE'S SICK?

TWEETMENT!

WHY ARE RIVER HATCHIMALS SUCH GOOD COMPANY?

THEIR CONVERSATION ALWAYS FLOWS!

WHAT DID TEAL BEAVEERY SAY WHEN RED SWOTTER ASKED IF SHE WANTED A SWIM?

'I SHORE DO!'

WHERE DID GREEN DUCKLE GO WHEN HE WAS FEELING UNWELL?

TO THE DUCK-TOR!

WHY DOES BLUE DUCKLE WATCH THE NEWS?

TO SEE THE FEATHER FORECAST!

WHAT DID RED SWOTTER SAY TO CONGRATULATE PINK HIPHATCH ON HER BIRTHDAY?

'HIP, HIP, HOORAY!'

48

WHAT DO BLUE DUCKLE AND GREEN DUCKLE WATCH ON TV TOGETHER?

DUCK-UMENTARIES!

WHAT'S ANOTHER NAME FOR A CLEVER DUCKLE?

WISE QUACKER!

WHAT DID THE DETECTIVE DUCKLE SAY?

'LET'S QUACK THIS CASE!'

WHY DID GREEN DUCKLE FLY SOUTH FOR THE WINTER?

IT WAS TOO FAR TO WALK!

WHO SAYS 'QUICK! QUICK!'?

A DUCKLE WITH THE HICCUPS!

WHAT DID BLUE DUCKLE DO AFTER SHE READ ALL THESE JOKES?

SHE QUACKED UP!

POLAR PARADISE

Polar Paradise is definitely the coolest hangout in Hatchtopia. After you've taken part in some eggs-treme sports on the ice, grab a mug of hot chocolate and warm everyone up with these jokes!

WHAT KIND OF HUGS DO POLAR HUMMINGBEARS GIVE?

BEAR HUGS!

WHAT DOES POLAR DRAGGLE EAT FOR LUNCH?

ICE BERG-ERS!

WHERE DOES POLAR SWHALE CATCH THE TRAIN?

AT THE SWALE-WAY STATION!

WHERE DO POLAR PARADISE HATCHIMALS EGGS GO TO THE TOILET?

IN AN EGG-LOO!

HOW DID POLAR SWALE MAKE POLAR SEALARK LAUGH?

HE TOLD A SWHALE OF A TALE!

WHY WAS POLAR SEALARK SAD?

BECAUSE SHE WAS BLUE!

WHERE DOES POLAR PENGUALA GO TO DANCE?

THE SNOW BALL!

51

WHAT IS POLAR SEALARK'S FAVOURITE SUBJECT AT SCHOOL?

'ART, ART, ART, ART!'

WHY IS POLAR SEALARK GOOD AT KEEPING A SECRET?

BECAUSE HER LIPS ARE SEALED!

WHAT DO YOU CALL A POLAR HUMMINGBEAR WHEN IT'S RAINING?

A DRIZZLY BEAR!

WHERE DOES POLAR SEALARK GET HER TAKEAWAY FOOD?

THE DIVE THROUGH!

WHAT KIND OF HAT MIGHT POLAR PENGUALA WEAR?

An ice cap!

WHAT ARE WHITE AND FURRY, AND HAVE WHEELS ON THEIR PAWS?

ROLLER BEARS!

WHAT DOES POLAR FOXFIN SING AT BIRTHDAY PARTIES?

'Freeze a Jolly good fellow!'

WHAT DO THE HATCHIMALS IN POLAR PARADISE LIKE TO EAT?

BRRRRRRR-ITOS!

POLAR DRAGGLE: Knock, knock!
POLAR SWHALE: WHO'S THERE?
POLAR DRAGGLE: BOO!
POLAR SWHALE: BOO WHO?
POLAR DRAGGLE: YOU DON'T HAVE TO BLUBBER, IT'S JUST A JOKE!

HOW DOES POLAR SWHALE BUILD HIS HOUSE?

IGLOOS IT TOGETHER!

WHAT DID POLAR PENGUALA SAY WHEN POLAR HUMMINGBEAR CHALLENGED HER TO A SNOWBALL FIGHT?

'BRRRRR-ING IT ON!'

WHERE DOES POLAR FOXFIN KEEP HIS MONEY?

IN A SNOWBANK!

WHAT SHOES DOES POLAR PENGUALA WEAR ON THE ICE?

SLIPPERS!

HOW DOES POLAR FOXFIN GET TO SCHOOL?

BY ICICLE!

WHAT'S AN IG?

AN ICE HOUSE WITHOUT A LOO!

HOW DID POLAR FOXFIN BEAT PURPLE FOXFIN IN THE HATCHY GAMES?

HE OUTFOXED HER!

POLAR HUMMINGBEAR: KNOCK, KNOCK!

POLAR FOXFIN: WHO'S THERE?

POLAR HUMMINGBEAR: HOWARD.

POLAR FOXFIN: HOWARD WHO?

POLAR HUMMINGBEAR: HOWARD YOU LIKE ICE CREAM FOR PUDDING?

WHAT DO YOU CALL A POLAR HUMMINGBEAR WALKING ON THIN ICE?

AN ICE BREAKER!

POLAR FOXFIN: KNOCK, KNOCK!

POLAR DRAGGLE: WHO'S THERE?

POLAR FOXFIN: POLICE.

POLAR DRAGGLE: POLICE WHO?

POLAR FOXFIN: POLICE HURRY UP, IT'S COLD OUT HERE!

LILAC LAKE

Lilac Lake is the ideal place to chill out. Tell a few purr-fect jokes here, and everyone will laugh so much they'll turn purple (except for the ones who are already purple from swimming in Lilac Lake!).

WHAT IS LILAC TIGRETTE'S FAVOURITE COLOUR?

PURRRR-PLE!

WHY DID LILAC Bunwee BUILD A new HOUSE?

SHE WAS FED UP WITH THE HOLE THING!

WHAT DID THE CARROT SAY TO LILAC BUNWEE?

'DO YOU WANT TO GRAB A BITE?'

WHAT'S LILAC AND SMELLS LIKE PAINT?

LILAC PAINT!

WHAT IS LILAC Bunwee's FAVOURITE Game?

HOPSCOTCH!

HOW DOES LILAC Bunwee TRAVEL?

BY HARE-PLANE!

WHAT DO YOU CALL YELLOW CRABLER IN LILAC LAKE?

LOST!

LILAC GIRREO: KNOCK, KNOCK!
LILAC SWHALE: WHO'S THERE?
LILAC GIRREO: ETCH.
LILAC SWHALE: ETCH WHO?
LILAC GIRREO: BLESS YOU!

WHAT DO HATCHIMALS CALL LILAC LAKE FOR SHORT?
LI-LAKE!

WHAT DOES LILAC SWHALE make in LILAC LAKE?
A BIG SPLASH!

WHY IS THE LETTER T LIKE AN ISLAND?
Because it's in the middle of WATER!

WHY DOES LILAC GIRREO HAVE A LONG NECK?
Because HER FEET ARE SMELLY!

WHAT DOES LILAC SWHALE HAVE AT LILAC LAKE?
A SWHALE OF A TIME!

WHAT DO YOU GET WHEN YOU CROSS LILAC GIRREO WITH LILAC HEDGYHEN?
A VERY TALL TOOTHBRUSH!

58

WHAT'S PURPLE AND RED AT THE SAME TIME?

AN EMBARRASSED LILAC HATCHIMAL!

WHY IS LILAC GIRREO SOMETIMES SLOW TO APOLOGIZE?

IT TAKES HER A LONG TIME TO SWALLOW HER PRIDE!

WHY DID LILAC PENGUALA CROSS LILAC LAKE ON HER BELLY?

TO GET TO THE OTHER SLIDE!

WHAT DO YOU GET IF YOU STEAL LILAC BUNWEE'S SHADY SPOT ON A SUNNY DAY?

A HOT CROSS BUNWEE!

HOW DO YOU SPELL LILAC BUNWEE BACKWARDS?

IT'S EASY: L-I-L-A-C- B-U-N-W-E-E- B-A-C-K-W-A-R-D-S!

GIGGLE GROVE

Giggle Grove is home to the
Giggling Tree, spreading laughter
and happiness throughout the whole of Hatchtopia.
Can you try doing the same with some of
these jokes?

WHY IS GIGGLING DRAGGLE SUCH A BAD DANCER?

BECAUSE HE IS TOO BUSY LAUGHING!

WHY WASN'T GIGGLING ELEFLY ALLOWED ON THE BUS?

HER TRUNK WOULDN'T FIT UNDER THE SEAT!

WHERE ARE YOU SURE TO GET A LAUGH IN HATCHTOPIA?

GIGGLE GROVE!

WHAT DOES GIGGLING PANDOR LIKE TO WEAR ON HER HEAD?

A PANDANA!

WHY IS GIGGLING ELEFLY SUCH A BAD DANCER?

BECAUSE SHE HAS TWO LEFT FEET!

WHAT DID THE TREE WEAR TO THE SWIMMING POOL?

SWIMMING TRUNKS!

WHAT KIND OF TREE CAN FIT IN YOUR HAND?

A PALM TREE!

WHAT DOES GIGGLING PANDOR EAT FOR BREAKFAST?

PANCAKES!

IF GIGGLING ZEBRUSH CAME UP WITH HIS OWN LANGUAGE, WHAT WOULD IT BE CALLED?

ZEBRISH!

WHY DOES GIGGLING ELEFLY NEED A TRUNK?

BECAUSE SHE DOESN'T HAVE A BACKPACK!

CLOUD COVE

Full of high-flying Hatchimals floating on clouds, this comfy hangout is great for unwinding and relaxing after a long flight with a joke or two, or three, or more!

WHAT DO CLOUDS WANT TO BE WHEN THEY GROW UP?

THUNDERSTORMS!

WHAT DID ONE RAINDROP SAY TO THE OTHER?

'TWO'S COMPANY, THREE'S A CLOUD!'

WHERE DO CLOUDS GO TO THE TOILET?

ANYWHERE THEY WANT!

WHY DOES CLOUD PUPPIT WAG HER TAIL?

BECAUSE NO ONE ELSE WILL DO IT FOR HER!

WHAT DID CLOUD PUPPIT SAY WHEN CLOUD KITTYCAN BEAT HER AT THE HATCHY GAMES?

'WHAT A CAT-ASTROPHY!'

WHY IS CLOUD PONETTE SO HEALTHY?

BECAUSE HE HAS A STABLE DIET!

WHAT WOULD CLOUD LEORIOLE USE TO ROW A BOAT?

HIS R-OAR!

WHAT'S CLOUD PUPPIT'S FAVOURITE SUBJECT AT SCHOOL?

BARK-EOLOGY!

WHEN ARE CLOUD PUPPIT AND CLOUD KITTYCAN HAPPIEST?

WHEN CLOUD COVE STARTS RAINING CATS AND DOGS!

WHAT SORT OF BOW CAN'T BE TIED?

A RAINBOW!

WHAT WOULD YOU CALL A LAMBLET WITH NO LEGS?

A CLOUD!

WHAT DO YOU SAY TO CLOUD PONETTE WHEN HE LOOKS SAD?

'WHY THE LONG FACE?'

WHAT IS CLOUD PONETTE'S FAVOURITE SPORT?

STABLE TENNIS!

WHAT DID THE CLOUD WEAR BENEATH ITS CLOTHES?

THUNDERWEAR!

WHAT IS CLOUD PUPPIT'S FAVOURITE TYPE OF PIZZA?

PUP-PERONI!

WHAT IS CLOUD PUPPIT'S FAVOURITE THING ABOUT HAVING A BATH?

USING THE SHAMPOO-DLE!

WHAT DID THE CLOUD SAY TO THE LIGHTNING BOLT?

'YOU'RE SHOCKING!'

WHAT DID CLOUD KITTYCAN SAY TO CLOUD PUPPIT THE FIRST TIME SHE MANAGED A HANDSTAND?

'CHECK MEOW-T!'

SNOWFLAKE SHIRE

Nestled in the mountains of Polar Paradise, there's snow place like Snowflake Shire! Hatchimals love to tell funny stories here, so join in with some of your own.

WHAT DO YOU CALL IT WHEN A SNOWFLAKE HATCHIMAL HAS A TANTRUM?

A MELTDOWN!

WHAT DOES SNOWFLAKE HUMMINGBEAR LIKE ON HIS FOOD?

CHILLY SAUCE!

WHERE DOES SNOWFLAKE SEALARK KEEP HER MONEY?

IN A SNOWBANK!

WHAT DID SNOWFLAKE NARWARBLER HANG UP IN HER HOUSE?

A SNOW-MOBILE!

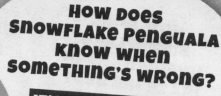

HOW DOES SNOWFLAKE PENGUALA KNOW WHEN SOMETHING'S WRONG?

IT'S A BIT FISHY!

WHAT DID SNOWFLAKE PENGUALA SAY WHEN A NEW HATCHIMAL CAME TO VISIT SNOWFLAKE SHIRE?

'ICE TO MEET YOU!'

WHY DIDN'T SNOWFLAKE SEALARK'S BALL BOUNCE?

IT WAS A SNOWBALL!

WHAT ARE SNOWFLAKE PENGUALA'S FAVOURITE LETTERS OF THE ALPHABET?

I C!

SNOWFLAKE WALWREN: KNOCK, KNOCK!
SNOWFLAKE NARWARBLER: WHO'S THERE?
SNOWFLAKE WALWREN: SNOW.
SNOWFLAKE NARWARBLER: SNOW WHO?
SNOWFLAKE WALWREN:
SNOW JOKE, I'M COLD OUT HERE!

HOW DOES SNOWFLAKE HUMMINGBEAR MAKE HIS BED?

WITH SHEETS OF ICE AND BLANKETS OF SNOW!

WHY DON'T THE MOUNTAINS AROUND SNOWFLAKE SHIRE GET COLD IN THE WINTER?

THEY WEAR SNOWCAPS!

WHAT STAYS HOT EVEN IN SNOWFLAKE SHIRE?

MUSTARD!

WHAT IS SNOWFLAKE WALWREN'S FAVOURITE DRINK?

ICE TEA!

WHAT IS SNOWFLAKE HUMMINGBEAR'S FAVOURITE PART OF THE SCHOOL DAY?

SNOW-AND-TELL!

WHAT DID ONE SNOWMAN SAY TO THE OTHER?

'DO YOU SMELL CARROTS?'

WHAT DID THE FURRY HAT SAY TO THE WOOLLY SCARF?

'YOU GO AROUND WHILE I GO ON AHEAD!'

WHAT DO YOU CALL SNOWFLAKE NARWARBLER WHEN SHE IS SKIING SLOWLY?

SLOPE-POKE!

SNOWFLAKE WALWREN: KNOCK, KNOCK!
SNOWFLAKE NARWARBLER: WHO'S THERE?
SNOWFLAKE WALWREN: SNOW.
SNOWFLAKE NARWARBLER: SNOW WHO?
SNOWFLAKE WALWREN: SNOWBODY!

WHY DID SNOWFLAKE PENGUALA WEAR ONE BOOT IN SNOWFLAKE SHIRE?

SHE HAD HEARD THERE WAS A FIFTY PER CENT CHANCE OF SNOW!

WHAT DO YOU CALL A SNOWMAN ON ROLLERSKATES?

A SNOWMOBILE!

WHAT DID SNOWFLAKE WALWREN SAY WHEN HER FRIENDS WEREN'T TAKING HER SERIOUSLY?

'SNOW LAUGHING MATTER!'

SNOWFLAKE BELUGULL: I JUST TRIED TO CATCH A SNOWFLAKE IN THE FOG.
SNOWFLAKE PENGUALA: WHAT HAPPENED?
SNOWFLAKE BELUGULL: I MIST!

WHAT KINDS OF CUPCAKES DOES SNOWFLAKE PENGUALA LIKE?

ONES WITH LOTS OF ICING!

WHY DID SNOWFLAKE WALWREN KEEP HER PIANO IN THE FREEZER?

SHE LIKED COOL MUSIC!

WHAT CAN YOU CATCH, BUT NOT IN YOUR HANDS?

A COLD!

WHAT OFTEN FALLS IN THE WINTER, BUT NEVER GETS HURT?

snow!

SNOWFLAKE BELUGULL: KNOCK, KNOCK!
SNOWFLAKE PENGUALA: WHO'S THERE?
SNOWFLAKE BELUGULL: ICY.
SNOWFLAKE PENGUALA: ICY WHO?
SNOWFLAKE BELUGULL: ICY YOU!

SNOWFLAKE PENGUALA: KNOCK, KNOCK!
SNOWFLAKE BELUGULL: WHO'S THERE?
SNOWFLAKE PENGUALA: SNOW.
SNOWFLAKE BELUGULL: SNOW WHO?
SNOWFLAKE PENGUALA: SNOW USE, I'VE FORGOTTEN MY NAME AGAIN!

MAGICAL MEADOW

With fun, fuzzy Hatchimals bouncing around the luscious Lullaby Grass, the Magical Meadow is the perfect place for spreading some laughter! Lie back, watch the clouds and tell these jokes with your hatchy friends.

WHAT DO YOU CALL A MAGIC HATCHIMAL WITH WINGS?

A FLYING SORCERER!

WHY DIDN'T ANYONE RECOGNIZE MAGICAL BUDGIBY AS HE FLEW BY?

BECAUSE HE WAS IN DIS-SKIES!

WHY DID MAGICAL BUDGIBY NOT LOOK SO GOOD?

HE WAS FEELING UNDER THE FEATHER!

WHY DO MAGICIANS LIKE TESTS?

THEY'RE GOOD AT TRICK QUESTIONS!

WHAT KIND OF STAR IS FLUFFY INSTEAD OF SHINY?

A HAMSTAR!

WHY IS MAGICAL PUPPIT LIKE A COIN?

HER HEAD'S ON ONE SIDE AND HER TAIL'S ON THE OTHER!

WHAT DOES MAGICAL KITTYCAN READ IN THE MORNING?

THE MEWS-PAPER!

WHAT KIND OF MUSICIAN DOES MAGICAL KITTYCAN WANT TO BE?

A PURR-CUSSIONIST!

WHY DID MAGICAL KITTYCAN CROSS THE MAGICAL MEADOW?

CLAWS SHE WANTED TO!

WHEN DOES MAGICAL HAMSTAR RUN AWAY FROM RAIN?

WHEN IT'S RAINING CATS AND DOGS!

WHAT IS MAGICAL BUDGIBY'S FAVOURITE GAME?

HIDE-AND-BEAK!

WHERE DOES MAGICAL HAMSTAR LIKE TO GO WHEN SHE VISITS OUR WORLD?

HAMSTERDAM!

WHAT HAPPENED WHEN MAGICAL KITTYCAN SWALLOWED A BALL OF WOOL?

SHE HAD MITTENS!

MAGICAL BUDGIBY: Knock, knock!
MAGICAL KITTYCAN: WHO'S THERE?
MAGICAL BUDGIBY: KOOK.
MAGICAL KITTYCAN: KOOK WHO?
MAGICAL BUDGIBY: DON'T CALL ME A CUCKOO, I'M A BUDGIBY!

WHY DID MAGICAL PUPPIT WANT TO KNOW WHAT THE TIME WAS?

BECAUSE SHE LIKED BEING A WATCH DOG!

WHAT'S THE BEST TIME TO BUY A BUDGIBY?

WHEN IT'S GOING CHEEP!

WHY WAS MAGICAL KITTYCAN A BIT SAD?

PAW-SIBLY BECAUSE SHE WAS IN A BAD MEWD!

MAGICAL FARROW: KNOCK, KNOCK!
MAGICAL KITTYCAN: WHO'S THERE?
MAGICAL FARROW: SADIE.
MAGICAL KITTYCAN: SADIE WHO?
MAGICAL FARROW: SADIE MAGIC WORD AND WATCH ME DISAPPEAR!

WHAT DID MAGICAL KITTYCAN SAY WHEN SOMEONE TOLD HER SHE COULDN'T DO MAGIC?

'KITTY CAN!'

WHAT DID MAGICAL BUDGIBY SAY WHEN IT TURNED COLD IN MAGICAL MEADOW?

'BRRRRR-D!'

GLITTERING GARDEN

With Eightlips instead of tulips and Buttercups dripping with real butter, Glittering Garden is the perfect location for telling a few sparkling gems! This is also where you'll find the Daisy Schoolhouse, which offers tons of magical egg-stra curricular activities.

WHY DOESN'T GLITTERING CRABLER PLAY TENNIS?

BECAUSE SHE'S AFRAID OF THE NET!

GLITTERING RHOOBY: KNOCK, KNOCK!
GLITTERING ALBASLOTH: WHO'S THERE?
GLITTERING RHOOBY: RHINO!
GLITTERING ALBASLOTH: RHINO WHO?
GLITTERING RHOOBY: RHINO EVERY KNOCK KNOCK JOKE IN HATCHTOPIA!

WHO IS THE MOST MUSICAL OF THE HATCHIMALS IN GLITTERING GARDEN?

GLITTERING PLATYPIPER!

HOW DO YOU GET STRAIGHT As IN SCHOOL?

USE A RULER!

WHAT DO YOU CALL SPARKLY JEWELLERY FROM THIS PART OF HATCHTOPIA?

GLITTER-RING!

WHAT DO GLITTERING GARDEN HATCHIMALS CALL SCHOOL TESTS?

EGGS-AMINATIONS!

WHAT DO YOU GET WHEN YOU PLANT KISSES?

TWO-LIPS!

WHAT DID GLITTERING CRABLER SAY ON THE FIRST DAY IN MARCH?

'PINCH, PUNCH, IT'S THE FIRST OF THE MONTH!'

WHY MIGHT THE TEACHERS AT THE DAISY SCHOOLHOUSE WEAR SUNGLASSES?

BECAUSE THEIR STUDENTS ARE SO BRIGHT!

WHICH SUBJECT DO OWLINGS ALWAYS GET TOP MARKS FOR IN SCHOOL?

OWL-GEBRA!

WHAT DID GLITTERING DUCKLE SAY WHEN SHE DROPPED SOME PLATES?

'I HOPE I DIDN'T QUACK ANY!'

GLITTERING DUCKLE: KNOCK, KNOCK!
GLITTERING CRABLER: WHO'S THERE?
GLITTERING DUCKLE: GARDEN.
GLITTERING CRABLER: GARDEN WHO?
GLITTERING DUCKLE: GARDEN THE TREASURE!

WHY DID GLITTERING DUCKLE BRING A LADDER TO CLASS?

SHE WANTED TO GO TO HIGH SCHOOL!

WHY DOES GLITTERING PLATYPIPER GET SUSPICIOUS AT LUNCHTIME?

BECAUSE THERE'S ALWAYS SOMETHING FISHY ABOUT THE FOOD!

WHAT'S THE SHINIEST FLOWER IN GLITTERING GARDEN?

A SUNFLOWER!

WHAT DOES GLITTERING DUCKLE SAY WHEN SHE TAKES A FRIEND ON A LONG, BUMPY FLIGHT ACROSS HATCHTOPIA?

'DUCKLE UP!'

HOW DO YOU STOP GLITTERING RHOOBY FROM CHARGING LIKE A RHINO?

TAKE AWAY HER CREDIT CARD!

GLITTERING PLATYPIPER: KNOCK, KNOCK!
GLITTERING WALWREN: WHO'S THERE?
GLITTERING PLATYPIPER: THANK.
GLITTERING WALWREN: THANK WHO?
GLITTERING PLATYPIPER: YOU'RE WELCOME!

79

CRYSTAL CANYON

Made of enchanting crystals that reflect happiness on everyone, Crystal Canyon is a joyful place. Tell these jokes and you'll be sure to keep everyone's mood happy and shiny!

HOW DID THE STICKY SWEET CROSS THE ROAD?

IT WAS STUCK TO THE BOTTOM OF CRYSTAL BEAVEERY'S PAW!

WHAT DO THE CRYSTAL CANYON HATCHIMALS SAY AT MUSIC CONCERTS?

'ROCK ON!'

WHAT DID THE STONE SAY AFTER IT ROLLED ALL THE WAY IN TO CRYSTAL CANYON?

'I'VE HIT ROCK BOTTOM!'

WHY IS CRYSTAL CANYON A GOOD PLACE TO LEARN NEW THINGS?

EVERYTHING'S CRYSTAL CLEAR!

WHAT DID CRYSTAL FOXFIN SAY TO THE FLEA?

'STOP BUGGING ME!'

WHAT DOES CRYSTAL CHAMELOON USE TO HIDE HERSELF?

CHAM-EFLAGE!

IF CRYSTAL OCTAPITTA HAD A BAND, WHAT WOULD IT BE CALLED?

THE ROCKTAPITTAS!

WHAT'S GLITTERING RHOOBY'S FAVOURITE GEMSTONE IN CRYSTAL CANYON?

A RUBY!

WHAT DOES CRYSTAL FOXFIN SAY WHEN HE'S COMPLETED A TASK?

'I'M FOXFIN-ISHED!'

81

WHO HELD CRYSTAL OCTAPITTA RANSOM?

SQUID-NAPPERS!

HOW DO YOU KNOW WHEN CRYSTAL BUTTERPUFF IS TIRED?

SHE GETS ALL PUFFED OUT!

CRYSTAL POSSWIFT: KNOCK, KNOCK!
CRYSTAL CHAMELOON: WHO'S THERE?
CRYSTAL POSSWIFT: A HERD.
CRYSTAL CHAMELOON: A HERD WHO?
CRYSTAL POSSWIFT: A HERD YOU WERE IN CRYSTAL CANYON, SO I CAME TO SEE YOU!

WHY COULDN'T CRYSTAL BUTTERPUFF GO TO THE BALL?

BECAUSE IT WAS A MOTH BALL!

WHAT DID THE SIGN ON CRYSTAL OCTAPITTA'S HOTEL ROOM SAY?

'THIS ROOM IS OCTA-PIED!'

CRYSTAL FOXFIN: KNOCK, KNOCK!
CRYSTAL BEAVEERY: WHO'S THERE?
CRYSTAL FOXFIN: CAN.
CRYSTAL BEAVEERY: CAN WHO?
CRYSTAL FOXFIN: CANYON!

CRYSTAL FOXFIN: KNOCK, KNOCK!
CRYSTAL BEAVEERY: WHO'S THERE?
CRYSTAL FOXFIN: CHRIS.
CRYSTAL BEAVEERY: CHRIS WHO?
CRYSTAL FOXFIN: CHRIS STALL!

WHAT IS CRYSTAL BUTTERPUFF'S FAVOURITE CEREAL?

BUTTER-PUFFS!

WHAT DOES CRYSTAL BEAVEERY SAY TO THE KIDS AS THEY HEAD OFF TO SCHOOL?

'BEAVEERY GOOD!'

CITRUS COAST

Time to relax in a hammock and fan yourself with Lime Wedge Leaves along the beautiful Citrus Coast. Tell a few jokes with your friends and wash them down with a Sunny Citrus Lemonade!

WHAT DO HATCHIMALS FROM CITRUS COAST LIKE TO DO?

JUST COAST ALONG!

WHAT DID THE COAST SAY WHEN THE TIDE CAME IN?

LONG TIME NO SEA!

WHAT DOES CITRUS NIGHTINGOAT SAY AT TEA TIME?

'BL-EAT UP!'

WHAT DID CITRUS BUTTERPUFF SAY WHEN HE SAW EVERYONE TIDYING UP?

'I'D BUTTER JOIN IN!'

WHAT DID CITRUS DRAGGLE'S SCHOOL TEACHER SAY?

'STOP DRAGGLING YOUR FEET AND WALK PROPERLY, PLEASE!'

WHAT DO YOU CALL CITRUS ANTEAGLE WHEN HE'S SICK?

ILL-EAGLE!

WHAT ADVICE DOES CITRUS MOOSEBEAK GIVE TO WANNABE STAND-UP COMEDIANS?

'YOU MOOSEBEAK INTO THE MICROPHONE!'

WHAT IS CITRUS NIGHTINGOAT'S FAVOURITE OUTFIT?

HIS NIGHTIE!

85

WHAT DID CITRUS FOXFIN SAY WHEN CITRUS BUTTERPUFF TOLD A JOKE?

'YOU JUST CHURNED THAT ONE OUT, DIDN'T YOU?'

WHY DID THE ORANGE LOSE THE RACE?

BECAUSE IT RAN OUT OF JUICE!

HOW DOES CITRUS NIGHTINGOAT KEEP WARM IN WINTER?

CENTRAL BLEATING!

WHAT DID CITRUS SKUNKLE SAY WHEN SHE TOLD CITRUS BUTTERPUFF A RUMOUR?

'YOU'D BUTTER NOT BREAD IT AROUND, THOUGH!'

WHY DO BANANAS HAVE TO PUT ON SUNTAN LOTION BEFORE THEY GO TO CITRUS COAST?

BECAUSE THEY MIGHT PEEL!

CITRUS BUTTERPUFF: KNOCK, KNOCK!

CITRUS MOOSEBEAK: WHO'S THERE?

CITRUS BUTTERPUFF: BANANA.

CITRUS MOOSEBEAK: BANANA WHO?

CITRUS BUTTERPUFF: KNOCK, KNOCK!

CITRUS MOOSEBEAK: WHO'S THERE?

CITRUS BUTTERPUFF: BANANA.

CITRUS MOOSEBEAK: BANANA WHO?

CITRUS BUTTERPUFF: KNOCK, KNOCK!

CITRUS MOOSEBEAK: WHO'S THERE?

CITRUS BUTTERPUFF: BANANA.

CITRUS MOOSEBEAK: BANANA WHO?

CITRUS BUTTERPUFF: KNOCK, KNOCK!

CITRUS MOOSEBEAK: WHO'S THERE?

CITRUS BUTTERPUFF: BANANA.

CITRUS MOOSEBEAK: BANANA WHO?

CITRUS BUTTERPUFF: KNOCK, KNOCK!

CITRUS MOOSEBEAK: WHO'S THERE?

CITRUS BUTTERPUFF: BANANA.

CITRUS MOOSEBEAK: BANANA WHO?

CITRUS BUTTERPUFF: KNOCK, KNOCK!

CITRUS MOOSEBEAK: WHO'S THERE?

CITRUS BUTTERPUFF: ORANGE.

CITRUS MOOSEBEAK: ORANGE WHO?

CITRUS BUTTERPUFF: ORANGE YOU GLAD I DIDN'T SAY BANANA AGAIN?!

WHAT TIME SHOULD CITRUS SKUNKLE GO TO THE DENTIST?

TOOTH-HURTY!

WHICH FRUIT IS GREEN AND SQUARE?

A LEMON IN DISGUISE!

WHY IS THE SKY SO HIGH?

SO CITRUS ANTEAGLE DOESN'T BUMP HIS HEAD!

HOW DO YOU KEEP CITRUS SKUNKLE FROM SMELLING?

COVER HER NOSE!

WHAT DID THE BANANA SAY WHEN IT BEAT THE APPLE IN A RACE?

BA-NAA-NA-NA-NAA-NA!

WHAT'S THE BEST DAY TO SUNBATHE ON CITRUS COAST?

SUNDAY!

WHY DID THE ORANGE GO TO THE DOCTOR?

IT WASN'T PEELING WELL!

WHAT WASHES UP ON THE TINIEST BEACHES OF CITRUS COAST?

MICROWAVES!

CITRUS SKUNKLE: KNOCK, KNOCK!
CITRUS DRAGGLE: WHO'S THERE?
CITRUS SKUNKLE: SHOES.
CITRUS DRAGGLE: SHOES WHO?
CITRUS SKUNKLE: SHOES ME, BUT I'VE HEARD ALL OF THESE JOKES BEFORE!

CITRUS DRAGGLE: KNOCK, KNOCK!
CITRUS SKUNKLE: WHO'S THERE?
CITRUS DRAGGLE: JUNO.
CITRUS SKUNKLE: JUNO WHO?
CITRUS DRAGGLE: JUNO ANY OTHER JOKES? I'M DONE!

YOUR TURN!

Now the joke's on you! Pick your favourite Hatchimal or Hatchtopia hangout and write a few funnies of your own on these pages. Can you make your friends crack a smile?

Running out of ideas? Use the words below to fill the gaps in these jokes, then write your own answers! I bet you'll come up with something hilarious!

DRAGGLE
EGGY
RIVER
MAGICAL
FLAMINGOOSE
RED
BUNWEE
SPARKLY
PUPPIT
SHELL
SILLY

CAMELARK
CLOUD
GREEN
HATCHLING
CHAMELOON
FUNNY
LAKE
ICE
WISH
RHOOBY
OCTAPITTA

WHY DID THE ....

HATCHIMAL CROSS THE

.... ?

....

WHAT DO YOU GET IF YOU CROSS A.................. WITH A.................. ?

....

WHAT DID.................. SAY WHEN THEY SAW THE ....?

....

PENGUALA: KNOCK, KNOCK!

TIGRETTE: WHO'S THERE?

PENGUALA:..................!

TIGRETTE:..................WHO?

PENGUALA:..................

..................!

ALSO AVAILABLE

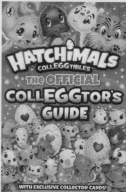